PUFFIN BOOKS

THE EYES OF THE EAGLE

Born in Kasauli (Himachal Pradesh) in 1934, Ruskin Bond grew up in Jamnagar (Gujarat), Dehradun, New Delhi and Simla. His first novel *The Room on the Roof,* written when he was seventeen, received the John Llewellyn Rhys Memorial Prize in 1957. Since then he has written over five hundred short stories, essays and novellas (some included in the collections *Dust on the Mountains* and *Classic Ruskin Bond*) and more than forty books for children. He received the Sahitya Akademi Award for English writing in India in 1993, the Padma Shri in 1999 and the Delhi government's Lifetime Achievement Award in 2012. He has now been awarded the Sahitya Akademi's Bal Sahitya Puraskar for his 'total contribution to children's literature'.

He lives in Landour, Mussoorie, with his extended family.

ALSO IN PUFFIN BY RUSKIN BOND

Puffin Classics: The Room on the Roof

The Room of Many Colours: Ruskin Bond's Treasury of Stories for Children

Panther's Moon and Other Stories

The Hidden Pool

The Parrot Who Wouldn't Talk and Other Stories

Mr Oliver's Diary

Escape from Java and Other Tales of Danger

Crazy Times with Uncle Ken

Rusty the Boy from the Hills

Rusty Runs Away

Rusty and the Leopard

Rusty Goes to London

Rusty Comes Home

The Puffin Book of Classic School Stories

The Puffin Good Reading Guide for Children

The Kashmiri Storyteller

Hip-Hop Nature Boy and Other Poems

The Adventures of Rusty: Collected Stories

The Cherry Tree

Getting Granny's Glasses

RUSKIN BOND

The Eyes of the Eagle

Illustrated by Priya Kuriyan

PUFFIN BOOKS

PUFFIN BOOKS
Published by the Penguin Group
Penguin Books India Pvt. Ltd, 7th Floor, Infinity Tower C, DLF Cyber City, Gurgaon 122 002, Haryana, India
Penguin Group (USA) Inc., 375 Hudson Street, New York, New York 10014, USA
Penguin Group (Canada), 90 Eglinton Avenue East, Suite 700, Toronto, Ontario, M4P 2Y3, Canada
Penguin Books Ltd, 80 Strand, London WC2R 0RL, England
Penguin Ireland, 25 St Stephen's Green, Dublin 2, Ireland (a division of Penguin Books Ltd)
Penguin Group (Australia), 707 Collins Street, Melbourne, Victoria 3008, Australia
Penguin Group (NZ), 67 Apollo Drive, Rosedale, Auckland 0632, New Zealand
Penguin Books (South Africa) (Pty) Ltd, Block D, Rosebank Office Park, 181 Jan Smuts Avenue, Parktown North, Johannesburg 2193, South Africa

Penguin Books Ltd, Registered Offices: 80 Strand, London WC2R 0RL, England

First published by Julia MacRae Books in the UK 1987
First published in India in Puffin by Penguin Books India 2013

10 9 8 7 6 5 4 3

ISBN 9780143332978

Typeset in Sabon
Printed at Replika Press Pvt. Ltd, India

A PENGUIN RANDOM HOUSE COMPANY

Chapter One

It was a high, piercing sound, almost like the yelping of a dog.

Jai stopped picking the wild strawberries that grew in the grass around him, and looked up at the sky. He had a dog—a shaggy guard dog called Motu—but Motu did not yelp; he growled and barked. The strange sound came from the sky, and Jai had heard it before.

Now, realizing what it was, he jumped to his feet, calling to his dog, calling out to his sheep to start for home. Motu came bounding towards him, ready for a game.

'No, not now, Motu!' said Jai. 'We must get the lambs home quickly.' And again Jai looked up at the sky.

He saw it now, a black speck against the sun, growing larger as it circled the mountain, coming lower every moment; a golden eagle, king of the skies over the higher Himalayas, ready to swoop and seize its prey. Had it seen a pheasant or a pine marten? Or was it after one of the lambs? Jai had never lost a lamb to an eagle, but recently some of the other shepherds had been talking about a golden eagle that had been preying on their flocks.

The sheep had wandered some way down the side of the mountain, and Jai ran after them to make sure that none of the lambs had gone off on its own.

Motu ran about, barking furiously. He wasn't very good at keeping the sheep together—in fact, he was often bumping into them and sending them tumbling down the slope—but his size and bear-like appearance kept the leopards and wolves at a distance.

Jai was counting the lambs; they were bleating loudly and staying close to their mothers. One – two – three – four . . .

There should have been a fifth. Jai couldn't see it on the slope below him. He looked up towards a rocky ledge near the steep path to the Tungnath temple. The golden eagle was circling the rocks.

Suddenly the great bird stopped circling. It dropped a few feet, and then, wings held back and powerful feet thrust out below like the wheels of a plane about to land, it came swooping down, heading straight for a spot behind the rocks.

The eagle disappeared from sight for a moment, then rose again with a small creature grasped firmly in its terrible talons.

'It has taken a lamb!' shouted Jai. He started scrambling up the slope. Motu ran ahead of him, barking furiously at the big bird as it glided away over the tops of the stunted junipers to its eyrie on the cliffs above Tung.

There was nothing that Jai and Motu could do except stare helplessly and angrily at the disappearing eagle. The lamb had died the instant it had been struck. The rest of the flock seemed unaware of what had happened. They still grazed on the thick, sweet grass of the mountain slopes.

'We had better drive them home, Motu,' said Jai, and at a nod from the boy, the big dog bounded down the slope, to take part in his favourite game of driving the sheep homewards. Soon he had them running all over the place, and Jai had to dash about trying to keep them together. Finally they straggled homewards.

'A fine lamb gone,' muttered Jai to himself. 'I wonder what Grandfather will say.'

Chapter Two

Grandfather said, 'Never mind. It had to happen some day. That eagle has been watching the sheep for some time.'

Grandmother, more practical, put in, 'We could have sold the lamb for three hundred rupees. You'll have to be more careful in

future, Jai. Don't fall asleep on the hillside, and don't read storybooks when you are supposed to be watching the sheep!'

'I wasn't reading this morning,' answered Jai truthfully, forgetting to mention that he had been gathering strawberries.

'It's good for him to read,' added Grandfather, who had never had the luck to go to school. In his days, there weren't any schools in the mountains. Now there was one in every village.

'Time enough to read at night,' retorted Grandmother, who did not think much of the little one-room school down at Maku, their home village.

'Well, these are the October holidays,' said Grandfather, 'otherwise he would not be here to help us with the sheep. It will snow by the end of the month, and then we will move with the flock. You will have more time for reading then, Jai.'

At Maku, which was down in the warmer valley, Jai's parents tilled a few narrow terraces on which they grew barley, millet and potatoes. The old people brought their sheep up to the Tung meadows to graze during the summer months. They stayed in a small stone hut just off the path which pilgrims took to the ancient Tungnath temple. At 12,000 feet above sea level, it was the highest Hindu temple on the inner Himalayan ranges.

The following day Jai and Motu were very careful. They did not let the sheep out of their sight even for a minute. Nor did they catch a glimpse of the golden eagle.

'What if it attacks again?' wondered Jai. 'How will I stop it?'

The great eagle, with its powerful beak and talons, was more than a match for boy or dog. The eagle's hind claw, four inches round the curve, was its most dangerous weapon.

When it spread its wings, the distance from tip to tip was more than eight feet.

The eagle did not appear that day because it had fed well and was now resting in its eyrie. Old bones, which had belonged to pheasants, snowcocks, pine martens and even foxes, were scattered about the rocks which formed the eagle's home. The eagle had a mate, but it was not the breeding season and she was away on a scouting expedition of her own.

The golden eagle stood on its rocky ledge, staring majestically across the valley. Its hard, unblinking eyes missed nothing. Those strange orange-yellow eyes could spot a field rat or a mouse hare more than a hundred yards below.

There were other eagles on the mountain, but usually they kept to their own territory. Only the bolder ones went for the lambs, because the flocks were always protected by men and dogs.

Chapter Three

The eagle took off from its eyrie and glided gracefully, powerfully over the valley, circling the Tung mountain.

Below lay the old temple, built from slabs of grey granite. A line of pilgrims snaked up the steep, narrow path. On the meadows below the peak, the sheep grazed peacefully, unaware of the presence of the eagle. The great bird's shadow slid over the sunlit slopes.

The eagle saw the boy and the dog, but it did not fear them. It had its eye on a lamb that was frisking about on the grass, a few feet away from the other sheep.

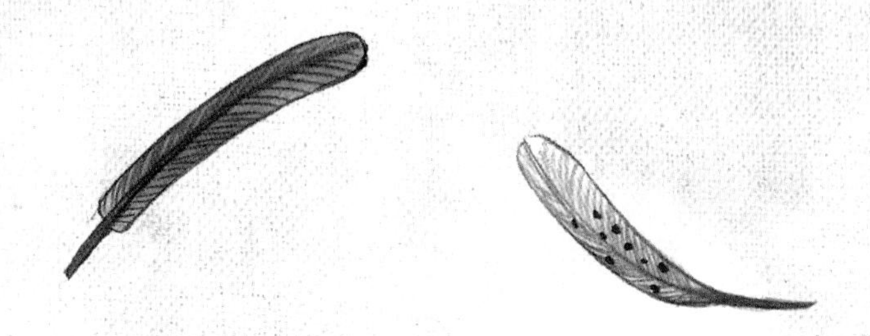

Jai did not see the eagle until it swept round an outcrop of rocks about a hundred feet away. It moved silently, without any movement of its wings, for it had already built up momentum for its dive. Now it came straight at the lamb.

Motu saw the bird in time. With a low growl he dashed forward and reached the side of the lamb at almost the same instant that the eagle swept in.

There was a terrific collision. Feathers flew. The eagle screamed with rage. The lamb tumbled down the slope, and Motu howled in pain as the huge beak struck him high on the leg.

The big bird, a little stunned by the clash, flew off rather unsteadily, with a mighty beating of its wings.

Motu had saved the lamb. It was frightened, but unhurt. Bleating loudly, it joined the other sheep, who took up the bleating. It sounded as though they had all started complaining at once about the awful state of affairs.

Jai ran up to Motu, who lay whimpering on the ground. There was a deep gash in the dog's thigh, and blood was seeping on to the grass.

Jai looked around. There was no sign of the eagle. Quickly he removed his shirt and vest.

Then he wrapped his vest round the dog's wound, tying it in position with his belt.

Motu could not get up, and he was much too heavy for Jai to carry. Jai did not want to leave his dog alone, in case the eagle returned to attack.

He stood up, cupped his hands to his mouth, and began calling for his grandfather.

'Dada, Dada!' Jai shouted, and presently Grandfather heard him and came stumbling down the slope. He was followed by another shepherd. Together they lifted Motu and carried him home.

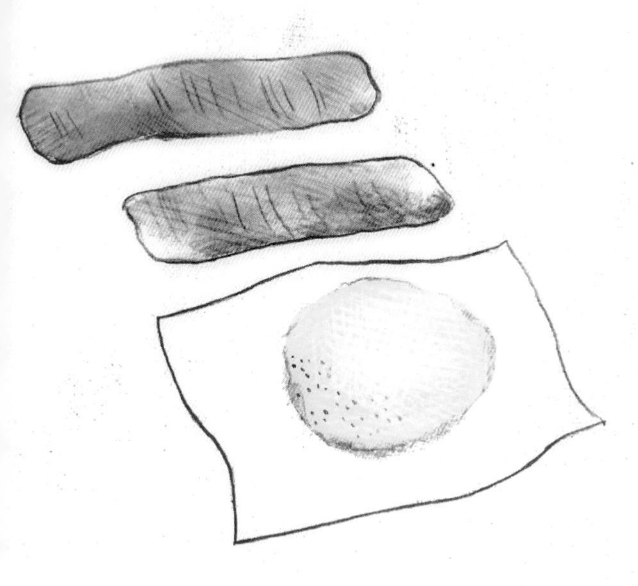

Chapter Four

Motu had a bad wound, but Grandmother cleaned it and applied a paste made of herbs. Then she laid strips of carrot over the wound —an old mountain remedy—and bandaged the leg. But it would be some time before Motu could run about again. By then it would probably be snowing, and time to leave these high-altitude pastures and return to the valley.

Meanwhile, the sheep had to be taken out to graze, and Grandfather decided to accompany Jai for the remaining period.

They did not see the golden eagle for two or three days, and, when they did, it was flying over the next range. Perhaps it had found some other source of food, or even another flock of sheep.

'Are you afraid of the eagle?' asked Grandfather.

'I wasn't before,' replied Jai. 'Not until it hurt Motu. I did not know it could be so dangerous. But Motu wounded it too. He banged straight into it!'

‘Perhaps it won’t bother us again,’ said Grandfather thoughtfully. ‘A bird’s wing is easily injured—even an eagle’s.’

Jai wasn’t so sure. He had seen the eagle strike twice, and he knew that it was not afraid of anyone. Only when it learnt to fear his presence would it keep away from the flock.

The next day Grandfather did not feel well. He was feverish and kept to his bed. Motu was hobbling about on three legs; the wounded leg was still very sore.

'Don't go too far with the sheep,' advised Grandmother. 'Let them graze near the house.'

'But there's hardly any grass here,' argued Jai.

'I don't want you wandering off while that eagle is still around,' said Grandmother.

'Give him my stick,' said Grandfather from his bed.

It was an old stick, made of wild cherrywood, which Grandfather often carried around. The wood was strong and well seasoned; the stick was stout and long. It reached up to Jai's shoulders.

'Don't lose it,' warned Grandfather. 'It was given to me many years ago by a wandering scholar who came to the Tungnath temple. I was going to give it to you when you got bigger, but perhaps this is the right time for you to have it. If the eagle comes near you, swing the stick around your head. That should frighten it off!'

Chapter Five

Clouds had gathered over the mountains, and a heavy mist hid the Tungnath temple. With the approach of winter, the flow of pilgrims had been reduced to a trickle. The shepherds had started leaving the lush meadows and returning to their villages at lower altitudes. Very soon the bears and the leopards and the golden eagles would have the range all to themselves.

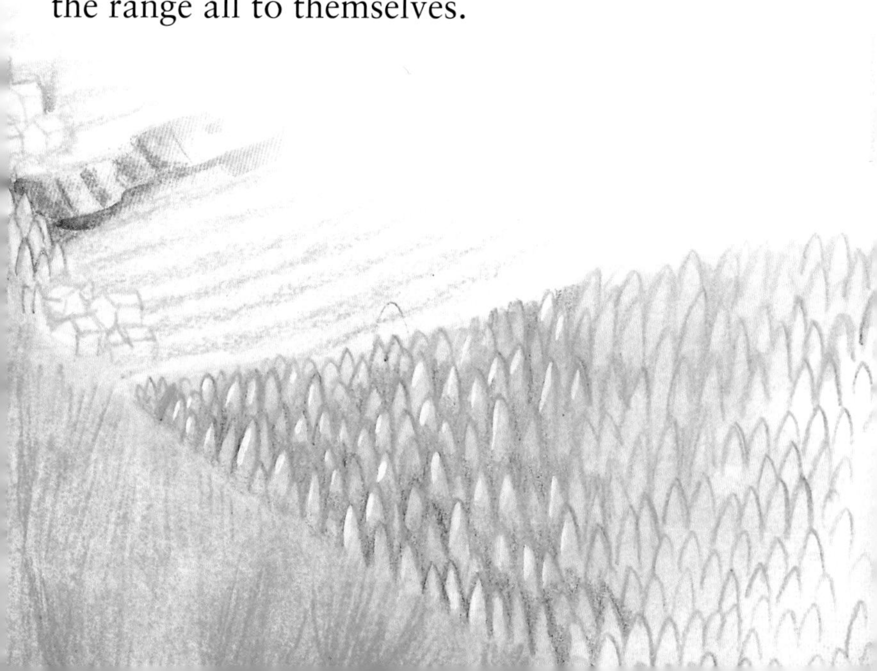

Jai used the cherrywood stick to prod the sheep along the path until they reached the steep meadows. The stick would have to be a substitute for Motu. And the sheep seemed to respond to it more readily than they did to Motu's mad charges.

Because of the sudden cold and the prospect of snow, Grandmother had made Jai wear a rough woollen jacket and a pair of high boots bought from a Tibetan trader. Jai wasn't used to the boots—he wore sandals at other times— and had some difficulty in climbing quickly up and down the hillside. It was tiring work trying to keep the flock together. The cawing of some crows warned Jai that the eagle might be around, but the mist prevented him from seeing very far.

After sometime the mist lifted and Jai was able to see the temple and the snow peaks towering behind it. He saw the golden eagle, too. It was circling high overhead. Jai kept close to the flock, one eye on the eagle, one eye on the restless sheep.

Then the great bird stooped and flew lower. It circled the temple and then pretended to go away. Jai felt sure it would be back. And a few minutes later, it reappeared from the other side of the mountain. It was much lower now, wings spread out and back, taloned feet to the fore, piercing eyes fixed on its target, a small lamb that had suddenly gone frisking down the grassy slope, away from Jai and the flock.

Now it flew lower still, only a few feet off the ground, paying no attention to the boy.

It passed Jai with a great rush of air. As it did so the boy struck out with his stick and gave the bird a glancing blow.

The eagle missed its prey, and the lamb skipped away.

To Jai's amazement, the bird did not fly off. Instead it landed on the hillside and glared at the boy, as a king would glare at a humble subject who had dared to pelt him with a pebble.

The golden eagle stood almost as tall as Jai. Its wings were still outspread. Its fierce eyes seemed to be looking through and through the boy.

Jai's first instinct was to turn and run. But the cherrywood stick was still in his hands, and he felt sure there was power in the stick. He saw that the eagle was about to launch itself again at the lamb. Instead of running away, Jai ran forward, the stick raised above his head.

The eagle rose a few feet off the ground and struck out with its huge claws.

Luckily for Jai, his heavy jacket took the force of the blow. A talon ripped through the sleeve, and the sleeve fell away. At the same time the stick caught the eagle across its open wing. The bird gave a shrill cry of pain and fury. Then it turned and flapped heavily away, flying unsteadily because of its injured wing.

Jai still clutched the stick, because he expected the bird to return; he did not even glance at his torn jacket. But the golden eagle had alighted on a distant rock and seemed in no hurry to return to the attack.

Chapter Six

Jai began driving the sheep home. The clouds had become heavy and black, and presently the first snowflakes began to fall.

Jai saw a hare go lolloping down the hill. When it was about fifty yards away, there was a rush of air from the eagle's beating wings, and Jai saw the bird approaching the hare in a sidelong dive.

So it hasn't been badly hurt, thought Jai, feeling a little relieved, for he could not help admiring the great bird. And now it has found something else to chase.

The hare saw the eagle and dodged about, making for a clump of junipers. Jai did not know if it was caught or not, because the snow and sleet had increased and both bird and hare were lost in the gathering snowstorm.

The sheep were bleating behind him. One of the lambs looked tired, and Jai stopped to pick it up. As he did so, he heard a thin, whining sound. It grew louder by the second. Before he could look up, a huge wing caught him across the shoulders and sent him sprawling. The lamb tumbled down the slope with him, into a thorny bilberry bush.

The bush had saved them. Jai saw an eagle coming in again, flying low. It was another eagle! One had been vanquished, and now here was another, just as big and fearless, probably the mate of the first eagle.

Jai had lost his stick and there was no way in which he could fight the second eagle. So he crept further into the bush, holding the lamb beneath him. At the same time he began shouting at the top of his voice—both to scare the bird away and to summon help. The eagle could not get at them now, but the rest of the flock was exposed on the hillside. Surely the eagle would make for them.

Even as the bird circled and came back in another dive, Jai heard fierce barking. The eagle immediately swung away and rose skywards.

The barking came from Motu. Hearing Jai's shouts and sensing that something was wrong, he had come limping out of the house, ready to do battle. Behind him came another shepherd and—most wonderful of all—Grandmother herself, banging two frying pans together.

The barking, the banging and the shouting frightened the eagles away. The sheep scattered, too, and it was some time before they could all be rounded up. By then it was snowing heavily.

'Tomorrow we must all go down to Maku,' said the shepherd.

'Yes, it's definitely time we went,' agreed Grandmother. 'You can read your storybooks again, Jai.'

'I'll have my own story to tell,' said Jai.

When they reached the hut and Jai saw Grandfather, he exclaimed, 'Oh, I've forgotten your stick!'

But Motu had picked it up. Carrying it between his teeth, he brought it home and sat down with it in the open doorway. He had decided the cherrywood was good for his teeth and would've chewed it all up if Grandmother hadn't taken it from him.

'Never mind,' said Grandfather, sitting up on his cot. 'It isn't the stick that matters. It's the person who holds it.'

READ MORE IN PUFFIN

Getting Granny's Glasses

by Ruskin Bond

Mani's Granny is seventy and can barely see through her old, scratched glasses. With only a hundred and fifty rupees in their pocket and a thirst for adventure, Mani and Granny set off to buy a new pair. On the way, they get drenched in heavy showers, run into mules and encounter a terrible landslide.

Will Granny ever be able to reach the town and get herself a new pair of glasses?